The Drama
of a
Single Woman

The Drama
of a
Single Woman

L.M. Grimes

To order additional copies of this book, contact:
Xlibris Corporation
1-888-795-4274
www.Xlibris.com
Orders@Xlibris.com
84842

Contents

For all women everywhere living the single life in the now or experienced the single life in the past. The moments of a single woman are to be remembered, to gain knowledge for the person she is now, and above all to be cherished.

"Some people are settling down, some people are settling, and some people refuse to settle for anything less than butterflies." – *Sex in the City*

PREFACE

B EING SINGLE IS a challenging world to live in. We have ups and downs just like all those relationships, madly in love with each other (of whom I am secretly jealous of) people, but our ups and downs are different. We have our own roller-coaster ride of emotions that we go through. If our roller coaster at a theme park had a name, it would be called the Twister, because it would have so many ups, downs, bumps, and loops with all the heart-racing and heart-wrenching turns and swerves that are involved. I wrote this book because there are so many single women like myself that do not get the love and respect that they deserve. I am here today to tell a story and to praise and say thank you to all the single ladies who have gone through similar stories as this one. I want to thank all of the men whose world collided with mine for the inspiration.

CHAPTER 1

Introduction to a Single Woman's Drama –
Welcome!

THE SUN WAS pouring through the spaces in between my blinds on a Saturday morning as I slowly awoke. I contemplate getting up and enjoying the rest of the day, until I realized how depressed I am still feeling. I slept in later than usual for a Saturday. The guilt of being lazy starts to consume me. I flip over and look at my alarm clock and see the red letters flashing out, 11:45 a.m. I cover my head with my blanket as I try and wish the world away, and then I slowly peak out beneath my covers, remembering who I am and what happened last night. I remember what happened that left me feeling this way. Knowing that this is not the first time and wondering why I keep putting myself through this. I met another guy who was a bad decision and another whom I am not important to anymore. A guy who waltzed right into my life and then he did a break dance right out of my life, just as fast. This left me feeling distraught, confused, and hurt.

I sigh to myself as I notice the mascara on my pillowcase, remembering the tears I cried last night. These tears would not stop no matter how hard I tried. Then a song comes to mind. Julie Robert's song of how men and mascara always run. "Did I give my love too soon or wait too long, did I take it a little too easy or put it on too strong. Last night, he said I was the one, oh but men and mascara always run." How true that song is right about now since a man (or shall I say boy, that is what I prefer to call men who treat a woman with disrespect) just broke my heart. He did not blink an eye. His actions were actions that he had probably done time and time again to other women. This is a game he plays in which he is always the winner at, because he always runs. A man who knows if he never commits, he can never get hurt. A man who hurts the woman before the woman has a chance to hurt him. A man who is afraid to love and is afraid to be loved is what he is. He did not think twice about his actions or about disrespecting me. He did not think twice about my emotions, my thoughts, aspirations, or goals. He was selfish and inconsiderate, and what gets to me is I let him be. I let him get away with the way he treated me. I let him hurt me. The sad reality is that I know I am to blame for letting him hurt me. I am responsible for me and my actions, and I let myself get hurt.

Last night was a fifth date, in which was my last with a man whom I thought had relationship-level potential. This was someone who I spent daydreaming about and envisioned spending time with. He was good looking, great personality, and made me smile. He said all the right words and treated me as if I was the only girl that was right for him. He was someone whom I thought could be a part of my life, someone whom I could picture being the man standing by my side. I drift off to dreamland, trying to avoid facing reality, and think back on all of the men who have broken my heart. I have run across Mr. Controlling, Mr. I Think I am Perfect, Mr. Selfish, Mr. Player, etc., etc. Not understanding why I meet all the men who want to break my heart instead of wanting to fall in love with me. Men that have issues truly loving me, caring for me, and who fall out of love with me so quickly. This leaves me feeling lost to what could possibly be so wrong with me that men do not want to share their life with me. This leaves me feeling like a failure when it comes to keeping a healthy relationship.

Then I awake again and realize that this is not helping me, dwelling on the past. Thinking about what happened last night will never get me up out of my bed. These thoughts leave me frozen yet time still ticks on and life is passing me by with every tick . . . tock . . . tick . . . tock. My head feels fuzzy and confusion sets in. I can feel my very being becoming more depressed as I stay frozen not budging, not moving, almost statue like, not, well, not doing anything. If I just lay here, not move, then nothing can hurt me. Men cannot get into my mind and hurt me. The world cannot hurt me. My bed is my safe haven. I wonder if I can just live in my bed for the rest of my life and stay happy.

Now crazy thoughts start to enter my head, trying to protect myself from the thoughts of last night. At least the crazy thoughts will keep the last night thoughts of bad memories away so that I do not let myself sabotage good relationships that I could potentially have. Now I feel crazy for thinking that my crazy thoughts are better than my thoughts of last night. Then, I make a wish that I could forget all the bad memories of the past. Dwelling on the past will only keep me in the past and hold me back from what I know could be one day. I try and go back to sleep so I can forget for just a moment longer of how lonely and how single I am and about my bad date last night with yet another frog. Another frog just hopped right out of my life and splashed water in my face, causing my grief and my hopelessness. Hoping he would be my Mr. Prince Charming did not turn out so well for me. I float back into sleep mode as I dream of finding Mr. Prince Charming and him holding me tight. I create a fantasy world in my head of how I would like my life to be with someone. If I cannot have the real thing, at least I can dream. My dreams are mine to keep and only I know what those dreams are. I can dream up Mr. Perfect since, of course, no one can take that away from me.

Mr. Perfect is someone who treats me right and wants to have a family. He is someone who likes me for who I am, does not try and change me, and we strive to make each other happy. Someone who is caring and is gentle in choosing words that could potentially hurt me during a disagreement. He is a man who wants the best for the both of us. He is a man who can put up with my ever changing emotions, and also know what to do for each of my emotions. Just like an emergency system. If the light is red, he knows to hold and support me. If the light is yellow, he knows to be cautious and respect the way I feel. Can it get any simpler than that? Of course, I have a bit more specifications than that, but it seems like there are no likely candidates waiting around the corner. No man that I am into, showing me a true concern of care. It seems like all the guys I am into, the relationship never quite develops into anything, and all the guys who are into me, I am just not all that into for whatever the case may be. Why does love have to be so difficult? And why does loneliness have to be a sad state of mind?

I can develop Mr. Fictional, so I at least have something to hold on to and to make the loneliness not seem so lonely and dreadful. Mr. Fictional is easier to deal with than Mr. Real. He is my drama-free man and the vision that I created in my head of how my perfect man would be. Mr. Fictional is there by my side making all my dreams come true. Mr. Fictional gives me a peace of mind to help me through the lonely days. There is nothing better than finding a man who likes to cuddle and keep me safe from the world. Someone to come home to every day, builds a family, and shares my dreams. Someone who makes me smile even when the day has been long and tiresome. For now, Mr. Fictional will have to do the job in place of Mr. For Real because Mr. For Real is nowhere to be seen as I look down my dark, cold, lonely, bumpy road. All I see is limbs, debris, and rocks in my way that I keep tumbling and falling on. I get up to brush myself off and start to make the steps down the road, only to fall yet once again. My heart is now bruised, beaten, tattered, and torn.

With that thought, I get more depressed with my single life. The word single is not a friend of mine. This is a word that I wish could be taken out of the dictionary to never be said by anyone else again. I hear a drum beating in my head to the tune that goes like this: Single . . . single . . . single . . . single. I start to feel the tears run down my tear-stricken cheeks. Great, now I am crying again. I never knew what rock bottom felt like with my journey on finding Mr. Prince Charming until now. I never thought at almost thirty, I would still be crying because of men. Two years of being single and going on dates has finally taken its toll on me. The single life has broken me down to where I no longer can hide from feeling hurt. Being lonely feels cold, dark, and causing a war to brew within the receptors of my brain waves. Now I truly know what being on the south side of lonesome feels like as Cheryl Wright sings. "I'm on the south side of lonesome and don't know my way back. I am confused, and I am broken, can't believe it hurts this bad, yeah, the south side of lonesome, you will know it when you get here if you haven't lost your mind."

Loneliness is a feeling that is hard to shake when there are no prospects knocking at the door. Waking up alone, eating alone, watching movies alone, and going to bed alone is something that I am told over time I will get used to and be accustomed to. Why can I not get used to being lonely? Loneliness is difficult to overcome the feelings of being scared that I might just be alone for the rest of my life. All of my friends and family who have a family that consists of a healthy relationship and growing children I envy and wonder what they think of me. I wonder if they view me as a failure because of that word that I am labeled as . . . single. This is an unpleasant feeling which leaves me being empty and living a solitaire lifestyle. A lifestyle that I do not want to be a part of, yet for some reason this lifestyle chose me and has a hold on me, and will not loosen the grip that loneliness has over me. Loneliness feels like an evil spirit who stays lurking around in the dark shadows. A spirit that is out of my reach and I cannot make go away, no matter how hard I try or do not try. A spirit that is not allowing me to move into the lifestyle called love that I so desperately want to be in. Hearing the word and feeling the thoughts of loneliness, motivates me to get out there to find someone so I don't have to endure loneliness any longer. But when I fail to find love, I am right back to my isolation feeling of loneliness. Love, the word is only four simple letters of the alphabet, yet the action of love is so hard and difficult to have. A simple word that sometimes is not so simple. A simple word, that causes a lot of sorrow, grief and tears.

I am scared of men in general. I am scared of my life changing when I meet someone, and I am scared for someone to change me. I compare my feelings to a terror movie, but instead my fear does not go away when the movie ends. My fear stays around to hold me back of the greater possibilities if I could just overcome them. Remaining in a frightful state of mind when it comes to me, sends alarm bells going off and ringing so loudly and high pitched that sometimes I miss opportunities because of the fear. The sounds of the alarm bells drown out any feelings of possibilities. My heart feels like an orchestra that becomes out of tune, after practicing for hours. The people playing their prized instruments become exhausted after a long day's work, just like my heart has. Exhausted mentally and physically to where I am not moving forward and I feel like a 4X4 truck stuck in the mud. The truck keeps spinning its wheels, and trying to reverse then forward, reverse then forward, reverse then forward. This cycle that will not end, no matter how hard the driver of the truck tries to make the vicious cycle stop. All of a sudden the driver then feels defeated and picks up the phone to call a tow truck. The tow truck then comes to the drivers rescue. I have yet to be rescued from the grueling cycle of loneliness and being scared.

Although I am lonely, scared and at my breaking point, I am content, stable, and independent right now for the most part, and I do not want to lose that. My independence is what has made me into the person that I am today. Although I do not want to admit it, I have grown a lot during this time of being single. I needed this time to grow and evolve into the person that I now am. I have now built a foundation and paved a way to be a person who has a better understanding and a better grasp on life. An independent woman who is good at what I set my mind to on every topic of life except for men. Men seem to be a down fall for me. Just like a waterfall that instead of staring at so beautifully in awe and from a distance, comes dumping a thousand pounds of water all over me and holding me down to where I do not have the strength to get up. I should be proud of myself and my accomplishments and not base my world so much around relationships. I do not want to be with someone that flips my world upside down and messes me up financially or emotionally, and that is why I am scared.

I try and not let a relationship define myself of who I am. After all, men do not make us women who we are. Men do not determine how we look or feel about ourselves. We are the only ones who can define who and what we really are. We all have a certain way that we want others to look at us. I want people to see me as a strong independent woman, not a lonely, pathetic woman who is destined to an eternity of aloneness. I do not want people to look at me in pity since I have been single for so long. I want people to see that it is okay that I am going through this phase of being single, and that it is a time in my life to grow and really become the person that I need to be. This is a time for me to make some accomplishments that I can be proud of and look back and be able to say, "Hey I did that all on my own."

I ask myself, what is wrong with me? Have I gained too much weight? Am I too independent that I scare men off? Have I been through so much that I keep running from men and will never settle down? There are many women around the world finding their Mr. Prince Charming, so why can I not find the one? Am I trying too hard or not hard enough? Is my path crossing the wrong men? Day after day, my questions go unanswered, so I wait for my turn. I wait for the day that I find the one who is going to be in my life forever. I wait . . . month by month, week by week, day by day, hour by hour, and watch the minutes tick away as time goes creeping by and as I start to get older and older. Do not get me wrong, I do not want just any guy. If that were the case, I would be married with five kids by now. Okay maybe not five but two and Mo (my small four legged fur ball, dog) running around and having the two-story house with the red door and white picket fence. I want that special man who cannot get enough of me, and he feels the same. I want that guy that I look forward to coming home to and sharing my world with. I do not want to settle for someone that I have doubts with or that might not be just the right fit in my life. So I keep on rolling down the road of being single until I find the man to give me that feeling to where I know I am with the one that is meant to be a part of my life. So as I keep rolling down the road, I hope that one day, the right intersection I will come to and I will slow down until I come to a complete halt and fall madly in love with Mr. Wonderful.

You know how some women say "I am done with men," but then they really aren't? They get over their bad date and decide they cannot live without Mr. Prince Charming. Then they get right back into the dating pool? I've been there many, many, and many, did I say many? Many times . . . But this time is different. This time I am done. I am no longer reaching for my phone to see if I missed any text messages, I am no longer thinking about that Mr. If I Can Only Make Him Mine. I no longer daydream about what it will be like to find Mr. Perfect. I no longer grab my lap top as soon as I awake to go on a dating site, the wonderful world of online dating, to find my next dating prospect. I am hurt, fed up with bad dates, lies and just plain worn out from the world of dating.

By now you are probably wondering how I got here if by chance you are not already here in the same place as I am. In this case, then you may know what the dark abyss of loneliness feels like. The waters are blurry and it is hard to even imagine that there is a light that will soon shine through, even if the light is just glowing dim. I am going on two years of being single. To some that is not a long time, but for me it feels like an eternity. These two years have become periods of my life that I am stuck in, and feels like I will not get past the single life. Being single does have its advantages, but being single for too long can cause a person to change in ways that people who have not been single for a long period of time could not even begin to understand.

This is a change that I did not sign up for or even ask for. This has turned out to be a change that has challenged every fiber in my body. For change to happen, I was the one who caused change and for my life to go from being in a relationship to now being single. I do not regret making those changes for those changes were ones that needed to happen for my health and well-being. Nonetheless, I caused the change and now to change my path again I have to put forth the effort to make those steps. Changes within life decisions are not as simple as picking out a pair of shoes to wear in the morning. Decisions that are life changing need to be carefully thought out and given time to nourish and contemplate to find the right solution. These changes caused the history of my life to take me down paths that I never would have imagined.

Now this is my chance to make the history of my life into something more, into the life that I have always envisioned and dreamed of. To look upon the past helps me to resolve mistakes I have made. If I cannot reflect upon my past, I will not learn from my mistakes and would possibly even re-live my mistakes all over again. My legacy is important to me, that I live an honest and respectful life, although, I would enjoy someone to share my legacy with. If I give up now, then I give up on something that is important to me. That something is a relationship with a special someone. A companion to share life's surprises, that life gives us. If I give up then I would not be giving my all. Giving up is not a method to the solution. This only creates despair and hopelessness. Giving up does not get me closer to my goals, only further away. There are so many obstacles to overcome. Obstacles are only pauses in my life. A pause for me to get through the obstacle, then reflect to make the situation better the next time around. So I continue to fight this battle of being single and to one day find the relationship that I am out seeking. My battle may become tiresome and fleeting, but at least I am working on conquering this soon to be defeat.

Everyone goes through different experiences in life. Experiences are a way that I can observe my life and what the next step should be. Being exposed to a variety of relationships let me know what kind of guy I do want and what kind of guy I do not want. Some people go from relationship to relationship and never have the down time of being single. Some have periods of being in a relationship and then being single. Others have been single for a very long time. Speaking to married friends, they all say, "Do not stress so much about being single, it will happen when you least expect it. The right man will come along when the time is right." Yes, when all that is probably true and good advice, yet sometimes annoying, it does not take away the feelings of missing someone to love within my life. It does not take away the want of having this need in my life that is almost as important as water or oxygen. Okay, maybe I am exaggerating just a little. I think that my wants in life should be explored so that I never look back on life when I am older, regretting not fulfilling a want that I had.

Single woman learn how to do things on their own that they normally would not have to. Single woman become more independent to where they do not necessarily even need someone. This is not necessarily a bad thing, because I learn how to do more for myself and take care of myself. The single life is like living in a different realm all together. Everyday can be different in the single life. Anything can happen daily in the single life and emotions are bouncing all over the place. Some days I feel lonely and some days are filled with wacky, yet exciting dates. People do not understand us. My friends who are in a long term relationship status give me the "I am confused" look all the time when at the beginning of the week I will be talking about one guy and then at the end of the week I will be talking about a different one. Sometimes I feel as if I am flawed because I do not have someone special by my side but flaws can sometimes be a beautiful part of what makes me who I am. Living alone can also be a challenge. Single women get so used to living alone – they almost turn into a different type of creature, an ordinary creature that they create themselves to be while living alone.

Dating, it is something that we all have done at one point in our lives to try and find Mr. Prince Charming. There are so many people out there with dating advice, guidelines to follow, and the right and wrong way to date. All of those thoughts and expressions boggle my brain causing me to not know the right way to date, or even if there is a right way to date. We experience a broad range of emotions, such as happiness, frustration, infatuation, love, hate, and stress. Many of us have had the challenge of being single longer than others and more often than others. So I ask myself, why is dating so difficult?

CHAPTER 2

My Mr. Prince Charming Pre-Qualifications

M Y CELL RINGS and as I am searching for where I placed it, I am wondering who could be calling me so late at midnight on a Thursday night. I then locate it in the bottom of my purse. Thinking of having an enjoying conversation with someone, I look at the phone number and roll my eyes. I think to myself, oh no, not again. Why will this guy not stop calling me? I told him I just wanted to be friends but he will not get the picture that I do not want to be with him. I went on two dates with this guy and he is obsessed. He remains so persistent in trying to talk to me. He thinks he can change my mind but no, not this time. I am not the one for Mr. I Know You Do Not Like Me, But I Will Not Give Up. I do not know if this guy is really that infatuated with me or if it is just the fact that he got rejected and cannot deal with being turned down by someone. Thinking back on the date of how he did not open the car door for me, how I paid for my own dinner, how he kept asking me question after question like I was on an interview instead of a date, and how uncomfortable I felt with him the entire night. I realize that I need to date with a purpose. A purpose that will help me reach a goal of finding a man that I am interested in. I need standards to follow. I need to have certain qualifications that a man must meet before I get involved. This way I am dating men who fit within the mold that I am looking for.

Pre-Qualifications for dating are tests that men must pass to captivate our attention. Pre-qualifications are like when a banker determines if a loan will be given based off of someone's credit history. The banker sizes the customer up and crunches numbers before giving out a loan. This is the same concept. If I have a list of deal breakers to follow and abide by my rules no matter how sexy the man might be, this will help me to achieve a relationship with someone who does not break any of my deal breakers. The banker, on average will not budge after running a credit check that turns out to be too low. The banker shakes his head and simply says, sorry but no. If I can say no to men who do not meet my pre-qualifications, then I will help myself to achieve better dates. Instead of going on endless dates that I wish would come to an end as soon as the date started.

We all have an image of what we are looking for in a significant other. We have a picture in our minds of how that special someone will act and look. A vivid picture that sometimes we distort so that settling for less suddenly becomes an option. Settling makes my image in my mind become only an imagination once I settle for someone who is not the image that I want. Settling for less than what I want does not put me in a healthy relationship. I do not want to settle for someone who does not make me smile, laugh and overall does not create a healthy environment. We all have wants and needs that we have in life. We all have certain needs that we just cannot settle for in order to make us happy. Needs are an obligation that I vow to follow. After all, living with the person I want to spend the rest of my life with is what matters. A lack of having what I need in my life leaves a part of myself that would remain missing and unexplored. I cannot always be pushing and shoving with the person that I choose to let into my life or that would make a relationship difficult. Too much fighting, yelling, and depression can create too much of a burden. A relationship is not supposed to be a burden or a feeling that brings me to a place that is unsettling. Do not get me wrong, I am not looking for Mr. Perfection, I am just looking for someone that I feel is compatible with me. No human is flawless and proficient at everything life has to offer. If I were perfect then I would be a super hero with super powers. If that were true, then being a super hero, I probably would not be going on two years of being single. I am just looking for someone who can fit into my life without complicating it more than it has to be. Having some pre-qualifications to follow will provide elimination of dating too many men who turn out to be all wrong for me.

I have established my dating pre-qualifications. We all have them in the back of our mind. What a man must do to meet our standards. They must qualify before we let them into our lives. Although the longer we stay single, our list shrinks, due to us settling or just trying to end the loneliness cycle, which is not the right way to find Mr. Prince Charming but the reason why so many of us settle for Mr. Wrong.

Settling is not the way to go for us to find our happiness with another person. Settling will create a heavy burden on my conscience. I am a firm believer that someone can be happy without being in a relationship. However, I have to stop dwelling on not being in a relationship if I am going to be happy with my life as a single woman. I would rather remain single than settle for someone who I may not love whole heartedly. With that said, if I am going to add someone to my life, I need to have that same level of happiness with someone else. But nonetheless, there are pre-qualifications that are important for my ideal man. Your pre-qualifications will probably look different, but read on to see what my ideal man pre-qualifications look like.

Finding Mr. Wonderful Pre-Qualification # 1

Mr. Prince Charming I must be physically attracted to. I am not saying this man has to be six feet, dark hair, and have rock-hard abs, since that man in love with me only exists in my dreams. A world that is not even close to reality. A world where my life would reflect a romance novel filled with love and passion. Although if I settle, then I may create a nightmare filled with horror instead of a romance novel. I am just saying if there is not some level of attraction to him, then the relationship will not work. Let me just be honest, if I am not attracted to someone, then I am not attracted, and the relationship will not work. Now attraction is not all about outer beauty because to me if someone's inner beauty is amazing, then the inner beauty will illuminate to the outer beauty making me attracted to someone. My ideal man would have good facial features, a rugged look, no six-pack abs (since I will never live up to that myself) also he has to be at least five feet six inches in height, someone who is slightly taller than my-self.

Finding Mr. Wonderful Pre-Qualification # 2

Mr. Prince Charming must open or at least attempt to open the car door/doors in general. A man who can still open a door for a woman shows that he respects you, wants to care for you, and still has traditional values. Respect is very important that I have in a relationship, someone who can value my sense of worth. If respect is not there, then that causes me to have self-esteem issues and to not like who I am. A man or a woman does not deserve to live that way or to be treated with disrespect or no regard to their significant other. Opening the door started way back when. I like to hold out hope that chivalry is not dead. This also refers back to mannerisms. Men who grew up learning to have manners and respect for a woman, usually treats her the way we women deserve. For some reason, something as little as opening a car door shows me that my man wants to protect me, and to me, that is sexy.

Finding Mr. Wonderful Pre-Qualification # 3

Mr. Prince Charming must pay for the first date. A man who pays for the first date shows a woman that again he can take care of her. Every woman, no matter how independent, to some degree, needs to know that her man can take care of her. The first date is the very first time for a man to make a good impression if he wants to see her again. If a man can show value in how he treats me from the beginning then that makes a big difference within how the first date will go.

Now after the first date, I like to split the cost of dates 50/50 or even surprise him by taking him out somewhere unexpectedly. Do not get me wrong, I am very independent and like to pay for myself, but that first date is the first impression for a man to make. If he cannot pay for that first date, then it is not going to work for me because that to me shows that he does not want to take care of someone and that he is in it for himself. Now with that being said, if a man that I am into is not financially stable, that is not a deal breaker, it just means we do something different for the first date, such as going to the park. And if a man invites me to his place for a first date that is a definite no, because that just means to me that he is going to try and get me into his bedroom, which leads me to the next pre-qualification.

Finding Mr. Wonderful Pre-Qualification # 4

Mr. Prince Charming must not try and do the bump-and-grind with me on the first date. This shows that the man is not interested in courting a woman through a series of dates before adding sex to the relationship. Courting a woman is important. This shows that the man, is truly interested, and gets to know his date before moving on to doing the bump-and-grind which creates a deeper emotional connection for women. Courting also shows that the man respects the woman he is with and respect is a big part of what I am looking for in an individual. If a man skips the courting part of a relationship then afterwards this can cause a relationship to be awkward. This can make a relationship tough to continue. Especially on the woman's part since women are emotional human beings and to most women, sex is a big deal and places a lot of value on sex. This type of man who wants sex on the first date is a one night man. Men who only want to date a woman once, has sex and never sees her again or only sees her for more sex which is using her and dating for the wrong reasons. Now men who want sex on the first date are not always like this, but most often this is the type of man that I find.

A man who tries to get down and dirty on the first date shows me that he is not serious about being in a relationship. Now with that said, I have never met a man yet to turn down doing the naughty, so if I initiate it, then that is a different story, but having sex from the beginning can be a definite turn off for either person. Because having sex before truly knowing a person can sometimes be meaningless to both individuals. I am looking for a man who has relationship-level potential when I date now, so this type of man will usually not get a call back from me if I sense that sex is all he is after. Let's face it, men and woman are human, and we like sex, sex feels good. Sex is a part of our human nature to want and enjoy. But men will take us women more serious if we hold out and wait for a more appropriate time. The, I want to be in a relationship with you level sort of timing. And if the man cannot wait for when the timing is more appropriate or sex is all he is looking for, then he is just a waste of my time since I want Mr. Relationship, which these days seem to be few and far between. If a man cannot wait until a woman is ready for that next step, then respect is not there. When respect is not there, this makes a relationship difficult to have with this type of man.

Finding Mr. Wonderful Pre-Qualification # 5

Mr. Prince Charming must give me a compliment. A man who can give at least one compliment on a first date shows that he is into me and knows that we women like to hear compliments every now and then. He is someone that is confident and wants to impress. He will ensure that I know he is into me by saying something that will make me smile and possibly blush. If a man does not give a compliment on the first date, then he probably will not give many compliments during the relationship. Some men are timid and do not give compliments, and there is nothing wrong with that, but this is something that cannot go missing in a relationship. But *beware* of Mr. Sweet Talker. Mr. Sweet Talker can talk someone all the way to his bed if you do not watch out. There is a difference between a man giving a compliment because he really likes me for me, and a man giving a compliment because he wants to do the bump and grind and that is all. This type of guy lays on the compliments thick and over exaggerates everything to get what he wants.

Finding Mr. Wonderful Pre-Qualification # 6

Mr. Prince Charming does not lie from the start. A man that lies from the beginning is a very big warning sign to *run*! Little lies, white lies, big lies, whatever kind of lies, are never good for any relationship. If he lies about his relationship status, such as he says he is single but really is not, do not waste time with Mr. Unfaithful and try to be the one to change him because usually Mr. Unfaithful does not change. Mr. Unfaithful will only break hearts and never stops because, for some reason, that is what makes this man happy and feel good. Do not get caught up with a guy that makes your self-worth feel small. Also if he is telling a story and the fish just keeps getting bigger and bigger, then that is how the entire relationship will always be. This type of person brings so much anxiety and stress to a relationship that is unnecessary. Mr. Unfaithful causes drama and chaos.

Finding Mr. Wonderful Pre-Qualification # 7

Mr. Prince charming must not be over bearing or too controlling. Since I have been so independent and grew up being independent I am not the type of woman who can be controlled and told what to do. I do think it is important to let a man be masculine and voice his opinions. A man who constantly tells me what to do all the time or always has a controlling tone makes me feel uncomfortable and a little scared. If I feel intimidated all the time by someone or feel that every aspect of my life is being controlled, this is not a way that I personally can live. Now being just a little controlling underneath the sheets is okay, but not on a daily basis. If a controlling attitude makes me feel small and worthless, then depression sets in and this is no way to live everyday life.

I am sure there are many other factors to consider, but these are my pre-qualifications for the first date that are important to me. We all have some sort of guidelines in dating to follow to find the one. Pre-qualifications are something that is important for Mr. Prince Charming to have. It is important to know what pre-qualifications look like, so we do not always feel like we have to settle for less. It is good to pinpoint what those are. The pre-qualifications should be major deal-breaker items and not the small quirks that we all have. If a man does not have a pre-qualification that is specified and a woman lets the pre-qualification slide, then just remember the woman has to live without that quality in the end. I cannot change the one I choose to be in a relationship with. I have to accept the man I choose for the way he is. If a woman finds herself always trying to change a man, then it is probably not the best relationship to be in. Women, let's admit it, after being single for too long, we do sometimes get desperate and will find ourselves settling until the poor schmuck drives us insane, and we have no choice but to move on. When we do this though, we most importantly lead the poor schmuck on and waste his time, but we also waste our own time looking for our Mr. Prince Charming.

CHAPTER 3

The Ex-Husband

I DO HAVE ONE of these, and a title of having to tell everyone from my doctor, to my insurance agent, job applications, the electrical company, that I am divorced. I have collected an ex-husband on my journey of life and men. I lived the married life for five years and then I lived through the whole divorce process when it came unraveled. I never once thought I would be a divorcee. I never once thought to be labeled as one of "those people." Divorce is tough because once everyone found out I also had to deal with the gossiping and judgments from others. Some were truths, and some were so far out in left field that the rumors could not be further from the truth. When playing house as a little girl, I never pretended to be divorced. I pretended to be marrying my perfect prince and having beautiful children. I pretended to be in love for the rest of my life. That is what I envisioned for myself. A blissful marriage, just like my parents have. They married young and are still happily married to this day. So I dream of what my future will look like as I grow older. I only think of the good memories that would come my way, as I should. Thinking of good memories and thoughts bring me positive energy and positive feelings in my life. I never intend for bad times to happen, but sometimes they just do. Sometimes life falls apart that I never would have imagined in a million years would fall apart. The bad times and the mistakes that I have made and will continue to make (since I am not perfect) help me to grow and to mature. I look at my mistakes as a learning curve and not as if I failed at something. Somehow I have to brace myself for the worst of times. Unfortunately, my divorce is an example of a bad time in my life.

On vacation, we went to Disney World. We stayed at the Shades of Green hotel where we had a wonderful time. We went to all of the different theme parks and had some great food. Especially at an Italian restaurant where my husband at the time and I talked for hours, like we had just met each other. In reality we at this point had been married for three years. We were sharing thoughts that drew us closer together. Everyone around us seemed to fade that night, with him being the only one in the world that mattered. This moment was a moment of being blissfully happy and in love. I could not wait to have more of these moments with him. But we fell apart. Something changed drastically from that vacation and to this day, I still do not know exactly what caused the change.

I met my ex-husband at a very young age. Mr. Ex-Husband and I got married when we were both nineteen. We met at the job we were currently doing, we were in different departments and units, serving our country in the military. We knew each other for about eight months before he proposed to me in Alabama on the gulf shores. We were very young and experiencing what love felt like. We were married for five years. He, originally from the north, and I, originally from the south, grew up in two different cultural backgrounds. He has the Yankee accent, and I have the country, east Texan accent. His side of the family liked to talk and joke about my accent, and my family liked to talk and joke about his. The wedding was actually entertaining as both families intertwined and mingled, learning from each other and the differences in how we grew up.

Mr. Ex-Husband is a great guy and handsome. Now you are probably thinking, wait a second, he is your ex-husband and you are speaking well of him? Yes, that is correct. I, to this day, still talk to him on the phone from time to time, but we just could not get along no matter how hard we tried. Somehow we both brought out the worst in each other, although we did love each other and I think in a way, yet in a different kind of way, we still do love and wish each other well. Have you ever had a friend or been in a relationship where you both just brought out the worst in each other? Got under your skin? Well, that is what we did to each other, and we both wanted to go different routes in life, so we departed ways. We both ended up being transferred to two different locations within the military and I think we both grew tired of the struggle to keep the marriage going. We both grew tired of the endless push and pull. No one was winning, yet no one was losing, and we could not settle on a tie.

It was tough to make the transition into divorce. Before we both got transferred to different work locations the divorce word started floating around, then actual divorce paperwork came about. I ended up moving out of our house and getting an apartment, while he stayed at the house. This was a decision and a time in my life that caused a state of depression that I hope I never have to endure again. We went through a lot of counseling, pain, and tears to save the relationship. There were good times and bad times within those five years. However, I do not like to dwell on the bad times. I like to try and remember the good times. We both knew that we could not stay married at the time, and it was for the best, but we both learned some valuable lessons on the lessons of marriage. Here on the next couple of pages are some of my valuable lessons I have learned within marriage.

Marriage Lesson # 1

I have to share, I have to share everything. All the way from the bed, the TV, the hammock on the back porch, the bathroom, etc. So how did Mr. Ex-Husband and I resolve this issue at nineteen? We got two of everything. Yep, we had two separate rooms for TV watching. We moved to a house that had two bathrooms. We even had two bedrooms if needed for those days that we fought, mostly over meaningless issues. Lesson learned: learning how to share is much cheaper, and we would have spent more quality time with each other if we were actually in the same room. Instead we allowed ourselves to live together while we lived two separate lives.

Marriage Lesson # 2

Learning how to develop patience with another person was a valuable lesson for me. Living with someone else helped me to start to develop endurance for situations that were trying on my nerves. Patience is very important in a relationship. Two people sharing everything and taking up each other's time, makes developing patience important in a relationship. There are times when I just have to bite my tongue from making comments. Such as when he is going slow and we are about to be late for an evening out, or when I had to sit through a movie that I did not find interesting. There were also times when I wanted to do a chore around the house for him because he was taking too long to do the chore himself. Developing patience with others helps to become a more rounded person by respecting others and realizing that everyone thinks differently than my-self. To realize that the world is filled with people who are different and accepting the differences is the first step to learning life lessons from another person. After all, that is one reason why we all are here living on this earth, is to learn from each other.

Marriage Lesson # 3

Honesty is another important lesson within being in a relationship. Honesty is the key to a healthy relationship. If one of us told a lie, then that key that once opened the door to our hearts started to wear and eventually stopped unlocking the door to our hearts. That is what lies do. After telling so many lies, a relationship can wear thin, making it more difficult than it has to be. Trust issues develop making everything the person who lied does, hard to believe when he or she is actually telling the truth. Everything becomes not what it seems, and all trust is lost. After this happens, a relationship is doomed for failure. Not only is the relationship doomed, lies also cause hate within our hearts and a rage that most people never knew they had in them can show through. Nothing good will ever come from lying.

I made the biggest mistake ever in my marriage when I was twenty-one. I was out one night with friends, socially drinking (a bit too much, acting as a 21 year old does when first turning 21), having fun, dancing, flirting with a random guy and he kissed me on the cheek. Not only did that weigh heavily on my conscience and tear me apart, but it also tore him apart when I told him. It was just one meaningless flirting event that meant nothing, however, it meant the world to how bad I hurt him and doing something that I never thought I would. There was also a time where there were rumors circulating at my work that he had cheated on me. That he was caught at the pool with another woman in a romantic way. Should I believe him or not believe him? A lot of people at my work did not know him on a personal level and had only seen him a handful of times so I was doubtful to if this was true or not. In that case, I actually chose to believe him after some time went by. We both were on the border of a dangerous road of cheating. We both knew there was an underlying issue of why this would come about. The issue was because we were not taking the steps that we needed to take to be happy and to remain in love with each other.

Everyone would like to think that marrying someone that captivates a person's heart will be easy, but marriage is not always easy. Marriage is a relationship that has to be worked on daily to maintain the future that the relationship holds. Somehow our relationship went from happiness to trying to make each other love one another in our own way that we needed to be loved. Because of us trying to make each other into something that we both were not, this is ultimately what caused our relationship to fail.

Honesty within a relationship can make a difference of a marriage falling apart or lasting a lifetime. Sometimes there will be hiccups in a relationship, but a relationship being strong enough to survive the hiccups is what can be the hardest. On the flip side, lies are never good. No kind of lie is good rather it be a white lie, a not the whole story lie, or what the other does not know will not hurt them lie.

Marriage Lesson # 4

Money is another struggling issue that couples face. This one is always a big one with a lot of couples. The key is finding a way that made our budget work and agreeing on how and what to spend our money on. We both had decent jobs at the time, making the exact same amount. When Mr. Ex-Husband decided to open up his own bank account without telling me, and I was the only one paying the bills out of the account that I thought both pay checks were going into, let us just say, that was a bad day when I came to this reality. Money is a topic that both people have to equally agree on how their finances will be handled to avoid this becoming a topic that causes arguments and grief.

Marriage Lesson # 5

Respect is an unspoken need that relationships need on some level. Couples have to have respect for one another. A marriage cannot lose that I want to help you and care for you attitude. If the relationship loses the level of respect that it started with, then the relationship will take a turn toward the worse that can be detrimental to the marriage. If two people have a deep found respect for one another, then respect will help them get through the tough times that life brings. Respect is not only important to show to one another while around others, but also when alone with each other. Respect is a need in my life with any relationship that I have, from a romantic relationship to a friend relationship and business type relationships.

There are times when I want Mr. Ex-Husband back. In fact I almost went back to him. I was down on my luck with finding a job after I quit from one that was not right for me and did not fit within my ethical standards that I stand for. So I almost hopped on a plane to live with him in Alaska until we talked on the phone and had a disagreement, and I realized why we divorced. I realized that nothing would be different. I realized that he and I are still the same head strong individuals that we were in the past and that life would be the same and we would soon be getting ourselves wrapped in the same situation as before. I also still had Mr. Friends with Benefits (in which you will hear about soon) as a distraction, so that did not help matters.

There are a lot of attributes I miss about him. Our separate needs were not being met since we viewed love in different ways and we showed affection in different ways. This caused a divide in the road which led us down the opposite paths instead of going down the same road side-by-side as marriage is intended. That fork in the road led us to lead separate lives, and to this day we both are still single and lost on our own separate road. Yet for some reason we both cannot explain why our roads will never cross. Sometimes I wish both of our roads would come to a four way stop, just so that I can see if we would both turn the same direction.

It is sad to say that in a situation like ours, where there was so much pain and tears, the outcome is probably best to leave the past where it belongs. Some attributes I miss about him are how much a gentleman he was, how much my grandmother loved him and still talks about him, and his dry sense of humor that somehow made me laugh. Now we both are in different times and places in our lives, and we both still want different paths in life. When we talk on the phone, there are times I remember why we got divorced and times that I wish he was still mine. I guess this situation between us, is a bitter sweet memory of him I will always have.

In the end, my marriage and then divorce helped me grow as a person. I definitely do not wish divorce upon anyone because it was one of the hardest moments in my life, leaving a good person whom I could not be with any longer because of the personality differences we had. A relationship is kind of like a puzzle piece. Two people have to fit just right into each other's lives to make it strive and grow. When two people are not striving and growing because they are not fitting together just right, then something has to change, such as in my case, the Big D had to happen. Marriage is a bond between two people that is very special. It is a bond that should never be taken for granted. So next time I get married (hopefully there will be a next time), I will make sure that he fits together with my puzzle pieces and that we cherish each day.

CHAPTER 4

The Ex-Fiancé

O N A COLD, SNOWY day in Minnesota where I was living at the time, I decide to go out to a bar where some of my co-workers were at. One guy, who was a coworker, who worked in a different department and unit, starts to talk to me. At first, I wanted nothing to do with this man. I thought that he was egotistical, arrogant, had a bad temper, bald, and not the type of guy I would ever be interested in. Something that night changed the way I felt about him. Could it have been the beer or could it have been true feelings for him? Either way, my world changed as I began to spend more of my time and energy with him.

Mr. Ex-Fiancé, well, I have one thing to say that one of my supervisors from work used to say when someone did something without thinking it through or making a bad decision – "That is just dumb." Yep, the biggest and dumbest mistake of my life that ended up changing the path in life that I was on. I was on a good path of staying in the military for twenty years, and then when my life intertwined with his, I ended up rearranging my whole life for a man who did not stay a part of my life.

Mr. Ex-Fiancé is not someone that I am proud to say I was in a relationship with. I am actually embarrassed to say I dated and got engaged to him. He flipped my world upside down and left me sideways. This man, I loved more than I have ever loved most. I loved him unconditionally. I loved his faults, I loved how he made me laugh, I loved how he could handle my emotional side, I loved him with a love that I hope one day I can find again.

But . . . a *big but*. . . this man hurt me more than anyone in the world ever or could hurt me. It was a hurt so bad that I would have traded the good memories in to not have to endure the pain that he put me through mentally and physically. So it leaves me wondering: how could I have ever fallen for a man of this caliber, and how could someone I loved so much be the one to hurt me the most? I still today do not have an answer for that question. I do know that I loved him so much and forgave him for so many wrongs when most people would have run, very far.

Friends, family, and coworkers looked at me with the what-are-you-thinking look, but I was so infatuated that I was blinded from seeing the real him that everyone else saw. A lot of people in my life knew that I was headed down a path that was not going to be in my favor. He worked in the same building as me, so not only did I lose the respect of my coworkers by dating him, but I also lost my self-worth of who I really was. My coworkers looked at me differently when everyone found out that we were dating. Dating someone you work with, even if it is allowed by the employer, is usually not a good idea. When you do that, you are inviting employers and other employees into your personal life by them seeing firsthand what is going on within the relationship. You also are judged by them, knowing who you are dating.

Here are some lessons that I learned from Mr. Ex-Fiancé:

Lesson 1: If a man has four different children by three different women, and all three have ill feelings toward him . . . *run!*

Lesson 2: If a man is going through a divorce with his wife at the time your world collides with his . . . *run!*

Lesson 3: If a man physically or mentally hurts you, and there is no end in sight . . . *run!*

Lesson 4: If a man is so controlling that you cannot go anywhere on your own . . . *run!*

Lesson 5: If a man is doing steroids . . . *run!*

Lesson 6: If a man cheats on you more than once, and most of his ex-wives are telling you that he cheated on them . . . *run!*

Lesson 7: If a man is selfish, and his needs come first over everything and everyone . . . *run!*

Lesson 8: If your life ends up mimicking an episode of the *Family Guy* because you are with a particular guy . . . *run!*

Get the picture? If a man cannot treat a woman as she deserves, then she needs to take off the blinders and get out before it is too late. Walking away was tough during this time that I was so deeply infatuated and could not see what was really going on. I ended up going off active duty for Mr. Ex. Fiancé to move to a different state, closer to where he was raised. Two short months thereafter I was lost with no-where to go, leaving him because of some terrible, unspeakable events that occurred. I think the last straw that confirmed to me that he was a perpetual liar was after I had left him and gone back to Texas. I was unpacking what few things I did take with me and found the receipt to the ring he had bought me when he proposed. The ring was in a Jared's ring box in which he said is where he had purchased it from, and he had told me the ring was really expensive, and it was going to take him years to pay. Well, the receipt told the truth. The ring he had bought from a military exchange for $436.00. Now if he would have told me the truth or not even told me the ring cost a lot or led me to believe that it was from Jared's, then I would not have cared since I loved him so much. But for some reason, he had to lie about every little thing. People judged me for being in this relationship, but I had to go through what I did to take a step back and say, "Hey, wait a second, this is all wrong." It was almost too late for me after a falling-out we had in regard to him cheating on me, again, but I was able to walk out of the hospital with some dignity left and start my new single life all over again. It was not easy, especially when I got involved with a manipulative man that took control over how I thought and felt. Some women have not been so lucky in life. No woman should put her-self in a position that she will regret later and will cause damage to her physically and emotionally for years.

Falling in the web of a bad guy is not worth all the pain and hurt it causes. Once you get twisted and tangled up, it is hard to break free. I still do believe that there are good men out there, and one will be right for me, I just have not had the chance to meet him yet, but one day I will. Just like other single women, we single, independent women, all deserve one. A relationship should be simple. Not fighting all the time, not pushing and pulling, but instead, having an undeniable love for one another. Life is already complicated enough. Women should not make it more complicated by being in a relationship that compromises her life. When someone drags me down, I know it is not where I need to be. Now there will be bad days of course, we all have our bad days, but most everyday should be loving each other and not trying to sabotage each other.

I want to live my days to the fullest. Every year I get older, and I want to look back when that year comes to an end and say, "Hey, that was a really good year that had some great lessons I learned from and some great adventures." After all, that is what life is – one big adventure for us to better our souls and to become the best that we can, so when it ends, we are ready and focused for the afterlife.

Because of meeting Mr. Ex-Fiancé, I do not take many risks with men anymore. I am cautious of whom I give my heart to and cautious for those men who want me for the wrong reasons. I may be too cautious at times and may have possibly scared a few men away because of it; this is something I am still working on. My image of men has been distorted because of my experiences with them, but I am hoping that one day the right guy will come along and can help me change that.

When people with good intentions end up dating people with bad intentions, it only spells *disaster*. I will never understand how I fell for a man that treated me so good yet so bad. All of these thoughts run through my head, with me trying to figure out why this man did what he did to me. Was he bipolar? Did he grow up learning to be this way toward women? Or just a selfish man who just does not have the ability to care for others? I have decided if I cannot understand something or why something happens, I will just let it go. I can sit and dwell and try to understand why something happened, but in reality I will never know. I will never know why he acts the way he does, but I do know that he was not right for me, and that is all I need to know. So the best plan of action is to move forward with life and stop looking in the past because there is nothing that I can do to change my past and going back in the past will only cause more turmoil. I will move forward and not backward. If I keep thinking of my past and let that take over my life, then the future will always stay the same. I will not ever move on. Grow and learn from what happened and go forward.

CHAPTER 5

Friends with Benefits

M Y FRIEND-WITH-BENEFITS, HE was a lucky guy to collide his world with mine. He did not realize what he was walking into when he met me. I was an emotional roller coaster that had an ultimate goal of finding Mr. Prince Charming, but instead I decided on finding Mr. Friend with Benefits. Sometimes I wonder what my brain is really thinking because as sure as none of this makes sense to you, it sure the hell does not make sense to me.

If you do not know, a friend-with-benefits is a special friend. A special frog who gets to be a person's friend, do the naughty with, and have no strings attached to him or her whatsoever. It is supposed to be a fun relationship with no emotional attachment. It has been medically proven that after having sex, a woman's body releases endorphins that causes her to have an emotional attachment with the person she chose to have sex with, so this phenomenon of having a friends-with-benefits almost never works for most people, including me.

After my ex-fiancé, who I also like to call Mr. Needs-To-Go-To-Sex-Rehab who shattered my heart into a million pieces, I decided to swear off men. I had in my brain that all men are jerks and that there are no good ones left. I decided to protect my heart and never let anyone else hurt me again. If I could just block out any sort of feelings that I have for anyone, then I thought my life would be better off than dealing with hurt and drama that men brought into my life in the past. So let me tell you how this chapter in my life began.

After my ex-fiancé and I were done, and called it quits, I realized I had absolutely no back-up plan and nowhere to go. I am sitting in my SUV and crying, trying to figure out where I am going, all the while feeling homeless. So the coin I flipped ended me up back in Texas, close to Dallas. One of my sister-in-laws helped me through my stay at the hospital and through my breakup process, and she suggested that I stay with her, my brother, and nieces until I figured out what I was doing with my life that had been shattered. She and my brother helped me heal by providing their home for me to stay at, company, and food.

A few weeks later, I was able to wake up, get over it, and move on. I got an apartment and found a job that was not my ideal job, but at least it was a job. The apartment I got was not much at the time since my minimum wage job I took on was not much at the time. After my healing process began and a couple jobs later (yes, it was a rough go), I decided to make my home there in Texas. To help me move on, I decided to start dating again, or at the least make friends in a new area where I only knew my brother's family. So I decided to do internet dating.

As I was doing my where-is-my Mr. Prince Charming search on the Web, I decided I also needed to find some friends. So I found a cool Web site that one of my, I-am-still-married-but-getting-a-divorce online dates told me about. It was a bad date, obviously, since he ended up still being married, but at least something good came out of it. This site has all types of groups within your zip code that you can join. Any type of group you are looking for, they have it. From work-out groups, sports groups, meditation groups, friends groups, dating groups, and much more. So I joined one of the all women groups so that I could make some new friends. That is when I met Holly. We were both single at the time, although she eventually found her Mr. Prince Charming. We hit it off real well. We had good conversations and laughed, a lot. It was good for me to meet another single female to talk about single life with.

One night we decided to go out for dinner and went bar hopping to have fun and check out the men. I mentioned to her how I did not need a man in my life and how I just needed Mr. Fun since I was still getting over the shock that Mr. Ex-Fiancé put me through. Well, Holly happened to know Mr. Fun who soon entered my life as my Mr. Friend-with-Benefits.

My Mr. Fun was hot and single. He was just a little bit older, okay, a lot older. Okay, okay, truth is told, seventeen years older. Yep, I was twenty-seven, and he was forty-four. He was completely all wrong for me, not the type of guy I typically date, but he was new, exciting, fun, and had me captivated. That is exactly what I needed or at least that is what I told myself . . . Mr. Fun was definitely that, especially the very first night our friends-with-benefits began. Now, ladies, be honest, have you ever had sex so good that no matter what that guy did to you, you will never forget that night? Well, I had exactly that. It was so amazing that I could have made millions on a movie scene for what we did that night.

Our date started out at the Taste of Addison. Very cool event where there was food, beer, games, rides, and music. Oh, did I mention beer? Well, because that is how I ended up in his bed. Mr. Fun and I knew that we were just going to "hook up" if things went well. All I have to say is things went well. So as the night went on and the beer went coursing through my body, we started holding hands and being flirty. He played his cards right with giving me compliments and treating me like I was the best thing to ever walk the planet. Before I knew it, I was in Mr. Fun's bed where I found myself waking up the next morning, and then the next, and then the next. Until I realized Mr. Fun was just that, and I got hurt when I fell in love with him.

Falling in love with Mr. Fun when I knew that he was Mr. Wrong was again a roller-coaster ride for my emotions. I started developing feelings for him when I was not supposed to since I was his friend-with-benefits. The problem was is that he did not fall in love with me. So I kept on thinking if I do this and do that, I can make him fall in love with me, but it was a no-go. Mr. Fun wanted to stay Mr. Fun.

After months of going back and forth from friends-with-benefits to I-am-never-talking-to-you-again, I found out that Mr. Fun actually had a relationship with someone else, and that is why he would not fall in love with me. Mr. Fun was really Mr. Jerk. I call Mr. Fun my enabler. As you can see, my Mr. Friend-with-Benefits has many names (Mr. Friend-with-Benefits, Mr. Fun, Mr. Enabler, I am sure I could think of more). We all have had an enabler in our lives at one point or another or we all have at least one all the time.

An enabler holds us back from moving forward with our lives even though we know the relationship is not right and it is not working. He as my enabler caused me to stay still and not venture out and go beyond this. This type of relationship caused me to put my life on hold, waiting for this person to become part of my life. Waiting for something that I knew was not going to happen. Mr. Enabler, I have come to realize, was going to cause me to lose a lot of valuable time in my life if I did not let go. I knew it was going nowhere, yet I was left stagnant and not pursuing or dating anyone else while he apparently was. If an enabler is bad for us, destroys us, causes emotional instability, then why could I not walk away? Why did I walk away many times and then go back? Enough is enough, I said, and then two weeks later, I was back with my enabler. Why did I choose to allow an enabler in my life?

Finally, I knew it was time for me to get past this. Somehow, someway, I walked away, for good. Mr. Fun taught me that there are men in this world that are only out for themselves and really do not care if they hurt someone. There are men who do not want a serious relationship, and that is fine, as long as they are open with this information from the beginning. I always want to believe that everyone is caring, nice, and means well, but that is not always the case. My Mr. Fun was overall a good guy, but he was so into himself that he could not see what he was doing to me and my life. He could not see that I was infatuated with him and tell me the truth so I could move on. Instead he kept it going until I finally walked away. So I finally broke it off with him, lost all contact for my own good. And then my life leads me on a dating spree.

CHAPTER 6

Trying to Be a Playa

A SLOW KISS AFTER a good date with a man who seems interested in me, he whispers in my ear that we should go back to his place. I hesitantly agree as I think to myself, none of these relationships last and he will eventually leave, so why not? Once we arrive at his place, emotions are running wildly and one thing leads to the next.

Yep, that is right; you read the title of this chapter correctly. Me, trying to be a playa while disarming men at their own game. I never knew I had it in me to stoop so low since this is definitely out of character for me. I decided since I cannot find the one who is right for me and meeting only jerks, that I would try something different and do what some men do.

Now if you do not know, Mr. Playa is a man who will treat you like you are a princess, then have sex with you and never call you. Or if he does call you, it is only because he wants to come back for more playing around, and that is it. He is a man who wants to be with more than one woman, or a man who does not want a commitment. He is only looking for sex for whatever reason or rationality he thinks that this type of behavior is okay. He could be single (let's hope) or he could be taken yet lie to you and tell you he is single (what a sleaze ball, I have a worst name for a guy like this, but I will try and keep this book PG-13 rated). That is the extent of a playa.

If people I work with, family, or even friends knew I was trying to be a playa, they would laugh. I am for the most part quiet and reserved, except maybe if I have had a couple of drinks (not that I drink a lot), and then a different loud personality comes out. They would probably ask me what is wrong with me or think I was not telling the truth. So you are probably wondering, why would you try and be a playa? What in the world could possess a reserved, decent-looking woman into this type of skill level? Well, let me explain.

Most of my dates, first dates, yes, the first date, ends up with the guy trying to get down and dirty with me. I often wonder why is this and how do these men find me? Some are really good at it and can sweet-talk a woman to where the woman does not even realize that she has just been talked into something. Others are bad at it, and it makes the date quite comical. How do I get all the horny, disrespectful, just-want-to-have-fun men? Do

I look innocent, easy, or desperate? Or am I just so damn sexy that they all just want to jump in bed with me? Well, I can assure you it is not the last one. I wish, but I am more of your average girl-next-door look. I cannot figure out this phenomenon of why all men want to bump and grind unless that is just how men are? This is an unexplained occurrence that I will never understand as a woman. I understand that they all have testosterone, and they all have "needs," or at least that is what they tell me, but so do women, and most of us do not look at jumping right into sex when we are trying to find love. So why do men?

Since I could not understand it, I thought, I cannot beat them, so why not join them? That is some smart thinking, right? Okay, maybe not so much. So I decided if men are going to be disrespectful, then I would be too, and I would play them before they ever get the chance to play me. That way I do not feel bad after a date gone wrong. So I beat them to the punch line and seduce them with my sexiness, get them in my bed or theirs, have a great couple of hours of foreplay (yes, that is right, foreplay). If I am going to do this and be a playa, then these men are damn for sure going to take the time for some foreplay. I then proceed to act hard to get and then do the naughty.

Afterward it is awkward because of barely knowing the guy, and then after a bit of small talk, I kick him out or leave, depending on if he is at my place or I am at his, and do not call him or at least try not to. That is how it works with men, right? But . . . there is a *big* difference. Men can do this with no emotional attachment. Me? Well, let me just say I was not a good playa. I would text the guy the next morning with "Why have you not called me?" Or "You're such an ass." Ah, being a woman means being emotional. Our hormones and the way we think are completely different from men. Due to these emotions, I obviously did not make a good playa, and not only that, I got absolutely nowhere except feeling worse than ever.

My self-esteem shrank and made me feel like someone who did not have much self-worth. I was too busy playing games and trying to prove to jerks that I could beat them at their game. While doing this, I was not only wasting time, but I also still had no boyfriend and no commitment, which of course was my ultimate goal. I was only hurting myself and risking my health by playing a game that I would never be the winner at. Treating life and people as if it is a game is never the best plan to go by.

Did trying to be a playa work for me? Absolutely with no doubt I can say no. All it did was put me back on board my emotional roller coaster that was always a dead-end road where I ended up still alone without my Mr. Prince Charming and without my happy ever after. So my playa days were short lived. This was a phase in my life that did not last long at all, thank goodness. I am glad that I came to my senses and realized that this was no way to live a good, respectable life.

I put down my playa gloves and instead put my bitch gloves back on and treated the playas that my world collided with the way they deserved. I told them what big jerks they were, cussed them out, deleted their numbers, and never talked to them again. Unless of course, I have one of my, I am-so-alone moments and one of them calls or texts me and I need some jerk amusement, so I answer back and mess with their head even though I know I will never see them again. I now know what these types of men look like and what type of allure they give off so that way I can ensure that I do not get caught up with this no-good-for-me type of guy.

In the end, the playa card is not for me. This period in my life did not last long at all. This was just a short stint of what not to do in the life of a single woman. This type of lifestyle is not what brings happiness to my life. This only brought negative energy, which made me feel bad about myself. When something in life is bringing me down and I know I am not living up to my full potential of who I could be, then that is when I know there is a problem and a change must be made for the better.

I never will understand how men or women can be a playa for long periods of time and be happy with themselves or their lives. This lifestyle definitely did not work for me when I decided to do my experiment. This type of person really needs to look within him-self or her-self to find what is missing to cause him or her to act this way. I just do not get how happiness can be derived from this type of behavior, but I guess everyone does have a different meaning of happiness.

Now back to the drawing board. Where will life take me next? I, of course, am not the type of person to sit around and wait for something to happen. I always have to be the one to do something about it and stay proactive. I always have to be involved in trying to make my life better and finding that special someone to share my chaos with. So now I have to decide which card to play next.

Contemplating on what my next move will be. I think maybe I will just do what all my taken family and friends tell me to do, which is do nothing and just wait because Mr. Prince Charming comes along when you least expect him. But no, I am not that type of person to just sit back. I have to take charge of life and keep moving. So then at that moment, the light bulb turns on shining bright. I know, online dating!

CHAPTER 7

The Internet Dating Spree

INTERNET DATING, WHAT a great idea! You can browse hundreds of profiles from the comfort of your home and set up a date to meet with someone. I call it the lazy way to date. Instead of getting dressed to go out in public in hopes of running into someone and striking up a conversation, you can be in your pajamas and wait for people to look at your profile and email you. Well, get ready to hear my adventures of Internet dating, and you be the judge to tell me if it is a good idea or not.

I browse through the many pictures of men on the online dating sites I signed up for. I sign up for the free ones of course since I have too much pride to pay to find a man. Although in the back of my mind, I know all the serious men are on the sites that have you pay to use their site. I respond to emails and start to develop some meaningful conversations with strangers. Again, in the back of my mind I am thinking to myself, this cannot be a good decision. Ignoring my thoughts I keep chatting away and setting up dates to meet some of the lucky chosen men to go on a date with me.

We shall start with Mr. I Am Married But Will Not Tell You That Online, guys. Yes, I said guys, as in plural, as in more than one. Their profile says single or divorced, yet when they get me on the date, they decide to tell me the truth, thinking that their good looks and charm will win me over and I will overlook the fact that they are married. I went on at least three dates with this kind of guy. After my third bad date, I got smart and started doing more research before I ventured out with online dates. I would go on their social media profiles online and see what their relationship status was on there, because if their wife is on their page, they will not lie there. Whatever their status is on there is usually accurate. You would think that they would be smart about their cheating and put their page on private, but most do not. These types of guys are the ones always seeking attention, so most attention seekers will not want their page to be on private.

Mr. I Am Married But Will Not Tell You Online number one was very cordial and nice. The first date, I met him at a Starbucks. The date was short, just to see what he really looked like and how his personality was. He was good looking and nice. I was digging him, so later on we have our second date and walk our dogs in the park. As we are circling around, having a good time, chatting away, and getting to know each other better, I mention that I have an ex-husband, and that is when I ask, "Have you ever been married before?" And then *kaboom!* He hits me with "Well, I am currently going through a divorce." I am polite about it and go, "Really?" I listen to his sob story and move on to the next conversation topic, while the whole time I couldn't wait until the hiking trail rounded back to my car so I could get in it and drive away. What I really wanted to say to him was, "What? You think it is okay to legally date when you are not legally divorced yet? You think it is okay to drag some new girl in the picture when your wife is still in the picture? This date is over." Instead I shied away from confronting him and never saw him again.

Mr. I Am Married But Will Not Tell You Online number two was a sweet talker and was young at heart. He was about the same age as me. And he actually became one of my friends after I told him I was not interested in dating someone that was taken. He was actually engaged to someone else. This one I met at the mall, and I walked around with him while he was looking for his "sister's" birthday present. Then after that we were talking on the phone a lot that following week, and I invited him to my house where we just kicked back and watched television. The following week, some girl calls me from his phone number. Thinking it was him, I pick up, and this girl is asking me who I am and this and that, telling me that this is her man, and I better step back. *Whoa!* I had no idea, and I was shocked just as much as she was. So this guy was the worst out of them all because he did not tell me. I had to find out from his girlfriend, yet I am still friends with him. Now tell me, how does that work? How do I remain friends with a total, complete jerk? No idea, but every time I talk to him, I respond with, "What's up, Playa?"

Mr. I Am Married But Will Not Tell You Online number three was another walk in the park. I like doing walks in the park for first dates because it has benefits:

(a) I get exercise and so does my dog Mo.
(b) The date can be short and out in public.
(c) The date is a relaxing first date. No having to dress up and be nervous.

So this guy shows up, good looking, very nice, and great personality. I am thinking, wow, this could turn into something great and, well, as you know how this is probably going to go, the exact thing happens as guy number one. *Kaboom!* Same bomb is dropped on me. I am thinking, wow, I am having a déjà vu moment, just with a different guy. He tells me how his marriage is not working and how he and she are no longer living together. So I tell him, sorry, I cannot date you until divorced, and he says he understands. Then, since I liked him, I give him the benefit of the doubt and go over to his house to watch a movie that same night. I think I was curious to know, and wanted to see that there were no signs of a wife still living with him. So I think I had a curiosity-killed-the-cat moment. So I go over there, and very impressed that there were no signs of a married woman living there. But I stuck to my guns and would not date him until he became single. So I have no idea what happened to him. He drifted out of my life once he realized that I was serious and needed to see those divorce papers first.

The all I want is sex, sex, dirty sex men. Yep, there was more than one of these; okay, I will be honest, many of these. So many I stopped counting. I will talk about a few that stood out. Mr. All I Want Is Sex number one took me to a nice Italian restaurant where all he would talk about was sex, sex, sex. He did not even look like your typical I-am-going-to-get-you-in-bed guy. He looked very reserved and even a bit on the dorky side. Even so, I could ask him how his day was, and some-how he would end up talking about sex. I was even slightly embarrassed every time the waitress came over and overheard his conversation about sex in some form or fashion. I thought maybe this guy just had an off night, so I went out with him again where we had a beer, but nope, it was all about sex again. So this guy had to go. He was a bit too horny for my taste for the first two dates.

Mr. All I Want Is Sex number two kept on trying to get me to come over to his house so he could try and have sex with me. Every date was him trying to get me to go to his house. The more he tried to get me in his house, the more it scared me and was a huge turn off. This one lasted through about four dates, and that was my limit with him.

Mr. All I Want Is Sex number three was a guy who tries to inhibit a woman's way of thinking with alcohol. Yep, he is the one that will buy you as much alcohol as you like and try to get you to keep drinking with the hopes that he will get laid. Date after date went like this, and all it did for me was leave me dehydrated with a headache the next morning. This guy stopped calling me. Probably because he realized no matter how much I drank, he was not going to get anywhere. I guess maybe his alcohol money was well spent on someone else.

Mr. I Do Not Look Like My Picture. People of course want to post the best picture he or she has on a dating site even if that means posting a picture that is five years old. Here is a rule for anyone who is or is thinking about doing online dating: post the most recent picture because it does no good to show what someone used to look like versus now. It only sets people up for failure on a first online date.

Mr. I Do Not Look Like My Picture number one was my very first online dating experience. You would think by going on this one it would have stopped me from my online dating spree, but not me, Ms. Proactive about finding Mr. Prince Charming. Well, as luck would have it, this guy was far from being Mr. Prince Charming. In his profile picture, he was a normal-looking guy with nothing abnormal. Then I meet him covered from head to toe in tattoos. Now do not get me wrong, I like tattoos, I have two, but I also like to see some part of the epidermis layer of the skin as well. He also had an eyebrow piercing, ears pierced and tongue pierced to add to his unique look. Now, ladies, this might be your type of guy, but for me, it definitely was not the type of guy I could imagine taking to an office party or even bringing home to meet my mommy and daddy.

Mr. I Do Not Look Like My Picture number two was a very nice man who ended up being about fifteen years older than he actually was. His profile picture was portraying an old high school photo and his age was a lot younger than he actually was. His car even had the old smell. To say the least, he was a nice, sweet, older man that was not Mr. Prince Charming.

Mr. I Do Not Look Like My Picture number three was a chef who had a goatee, and he definitely did not have a goatee in his picture. He was also a bit heavier than average in which his profile stated. Although he did not look like his picture, he was not a man that was out of the question until he started talking bad about

Texas since he was originally not from the state. Once he did that, there was no going back to him. Do not mess with where I am from, mister, and that brings me to the next set of men.

Mr. I Live In Your State But Hate It. *Huh?* Yeah, that is what I said. I went on two different dates, and these two men were talking bad about Texas – in which one was the chef mentioned above. Men should know these simple rules:

1) "Do not mess with Texas."
2) Why the heck do you live in this state? A man should not talk bad about the place that his date was born and lives in.

Get up on out of here, but most importantly this date is over. I guess it is typical to get this if you live near a big city in which I live right outside of Dallas, Texas (Go Cowboys!). But still, for me, there is no excuse for this.

Mr. I Am So Rich That All I Can Do Is Talk About Myself. There are a lot of women who set out looking for this guy. The kind of guy that has a lot of money, so in turn, she can be rich. But this, unfortunately, most of the time will not bring a woman to everlasting love or Mr. Prince Charming. These types of men rub me the wrong way. Usually I piss them off before ever going out on a first date with this type of man. Usually they will start the phone conversation by, "So do you own your own house?" and I respond, "No, I live in an apartment." Their response, "Oh, well, I live in a five-bedroom, two-story house, and drive a Lexus." I can almost hear the silent "So ah, I have more than you" added to the end of that because I know that is exactly what he is thinking. Do not get me wrong, it would be nice to find a guy that is financially stable, but it is like trying to find the needle in the haystack. I am hoping that it is not impossible to find the one to where money and possessions has not gone to his head yet.

Mr. You Are Great, But I Am Just Not That Into You. There are so many nice and sweet guys that I have been on dates with, but the problem is that I am just not that into them. I know I cannot settle, and I have to find what I want, so I have to let down this type of guy and tell him so. That is the hard part – when I actually meet a guy that is really sweet, but it just will not work out unless my heart and emotions are into it. I have to remember to think not only with my heart, but with my mind as well. Addressing all doubts will keep a healthy relationship. So I have to let these men go and hope that they find what they are looking for because they as well deserve to find their happy ever after. I ensure that I acknowledge my feelings and tell the person I am dating how I feel. If feelings go unknown, then I am not being honest with myself and the other person. I must remember to think not only with my heart, but also my mind, and if I have any doubts about something, address them with him, because doubts kill relationships.

Mr. I Love You On The First Date. Wow, am I really that good to make a man say I love you on the very first date? Well, apparently I am unless he says it to all women on the first date. Was that supposed to turn me on? It was a typical first date. We went to dinner to Applebee's, and he tells me he loves me then texts me after the date to tell me that he loves me. I never knew Applebee's was so romantic that a guy would confess his love to me over fajita wraps. (Let me guess, my next date is going to be at Chili's, enjoying Buffalo wings with a man proposing to me). During the date, he got a hug from me, and that was all. To say the least, the Mr. I Love You Man did not get a text back because, well, that was just scary.

As you can see, I went on a lot of dates where I met men online. As you can also see, it did not work out so well for me. Sometimes I will get bored and need a good laugh, so I will take my profile off hidden and go out on a date. I do it to kill time. Talking about killing, women, please be very cautious as myself if you do online dating. Make sure to talk to the guy on the phone first as a pre-interview then meet him in a public place. Also, consider doing the web camera before a date. This helps to verify the man is who he says he is in most cases. Never get into his car on the first-time meeting and never invite him over or go to his place on the first date. I know people that have met the love of their life by doing online dating, but so far this has not been a success story for me.

CHAPTER 8

Still No Baby

WHILE ON VACATION visiting my family, I walk into my parent's kitchen and see my four year old niece sitting alone at the breakfast table with a huge bowl of cheerios spilled into the bowl and all around it. No milk and no spoon, just cheerios. She does not realize it, but I see how content she is in that very moment with her cheerios that she managed to get all by herself. She was able to get the box out of the cabinet, get a bowl, and fix a snack for herself all on her own. I wonder to myself if she felt that she had made an achievement and was ecstatic inside. Nonetheless, I was very proud of her as I slowly turn my head through the kitchen door to watch. I amusedly watch her scoop a handful of cheerios into her mouth without a bit of grace. I smile at her, and then she notices me. She caught me looking at her as our eyes meet each other's. She freezes in mid cheerio scoop and looks around wondering if she is going to get in trouble. She all of a sudden gets the worried look upon her face. Then I burst out in laughter and she gives me a big beautiful grin with her big blue eyes and starts to laugh with me. She now realizes that I am not going to be upset with her and goes back to eating her Cheerios. She then sweetly asks if I want some. I snap a picture because of this being a memory that I would want to look back on. I sit down and enjoy some cheerios with her. I follow her lead and eat the cheerios just like her, with no spoon and no milk. She is so innocent, so beautiful, and so carefree, just as a child should be. I then think of all my nieces and nephews and how they all are such sweet and wonderful children and wonder when my chance will come, or if my chance to have a child will ever come.

Giving birth to a child is a special time in any woman's life – a time that is truly amazing and cherished. To give life to another human being is truly a wonderful experience for women. I, however, have not had this opportunity in my life yet. I commend all the mothers out there that have already had this special moment to give birth and raise a child – to take care of a child from birth, all the way through their teenage years. Taking care of a child is such a wonderful part of life, but having a child also is a lot of praying and hard work at the same time. Women are truly amazing beings. We not only make a living for ourselves, but we also take care of our special little people in our lives. I am still waiting for my time to come to give birth and to really relate to the wonderful mothers out there. This is a moment in life that I hope to one day have. Having a baby is a wonderful, beautiful, and rewarding time in a woman's life. There are steps to having a baby.

Step 1: Find that special someone to be in a committed relationship.
Step 2: Get engaged, then marriage.
Step 3: Start building my life with that special someone with special alone time and get used to living with one another in the married life.
Step 4: Try and conceive.

There are lots of steps involved to bring a child into this world, unless of course it happens on accident. Or a couple decides not to follow the guidelines that society has set in which I find nothing wrong with that. However, in following the steps, are all of them necessary? Has society now created a way for us independent women to skip these steps so that having a baby is much easier? Has medical technologies evolved so well that we now have other options? I ask myself, do I really need a man to have a baby? Well, nowadays the answer is actually, no. There are other options such as adoption, foster parent, or sperm insemination. I have always wanted a child but have not had that opportunity just yet, since I am single. One day I hope child bearing will happen for me. Maybe that is why I have been in a hurry to be proactive and find a man. Okay, truth is told that is why. I feel like valuable time is passing me by, and I am getting older by the second. With time not on my side, this becomes very stressful to not be involved in a relationship and have a want of wanting a child. So not only do I have to find a good man, but I also have to find a good man that wants children or wants more children depending on if he already has some or not.

Why do most women want babies? Having a baby is a maternal instinct. It is a feeling, a want for most women. When a woman cannot have a baby because of either not having a relationship or other medical reasons, this can be a tough situation to come to terms with. I definitely have not come to terms with the fact that it may never happen for me. So then my proactive mode turns on, and I think of other ways I can have a child without a Mr. Prince

Charming. Women do have other options that do not have a man to have a baby with. Artificial insemination, adoption, or to be a foster parent are three options. I have thought about artificial insemination before. This is where you go to a sperm bank and pick out a donor. For me I have decided against this, since I do want my child knowing his or her father and interacting with his or her father. Unless of course; artificial insemination becomes my last resort. Adoption is something that would be great – adopting a child that really needs a good home to live in, but it is very expensive. Being a foster parent is something that I would love to do – to take care of a child whose parent cannot care for him or her at a given time period. The only hard part for me is when the time would come for the child to go back to his or her parents. Realizing there are other options for me does give me a peace of mind, but it is still stressful letting go of wanting to have my own child to raise, nurture, and take care of for the rest of his or her life.

Before I started working the job I have now, I was babysitting for about seven families, part time. So I got to have the child interaction through my part-time job that I am missing from my life. I was making extra money while getting to spend time with children that are different ages and learning their characteristics. So I should be well prepared when and if my chance to be a mother comes around. I started babysitting part time when I was in between jobs and did not have much money coming in. I made a Web site, and I marketed it on different babysitting Web sites and found seven families who needed me. Now that I have a full-time job, I am only babysitting on occasion when the families I was babysitting for cannot find someone else.

I know that I will be a good mother. I cannot wait to have someone to care for and just be a mother and raise a precious life. I know that there is still hope for me to find Mr. Prince Charming, but I also know trying to find Mr. Prince Charming for the wrong reasons will lead me to Mr. Settling, which is something that I do not want to do because it will not lead to happiness. Also if I rush to try and find Mr. Prince Charming, then I will also appear as desperate, and no guy wants a desperate woman. That is not a quality that men seek out to find in a woman. The fear of running out of time must be overcome. Because if it is not, it can also cause crazy acting out, such as being promiscuous just to try and get pregnant and not caring who the father is. This is definitely not a road I want to go down. This will only lead to a custody battle and court papers and added stress. I have decided that if I am not on the road to having a relationship by the time I am thirty, then I will consider other alternative options such as, sperm insemination where a medical professional takes frozen sperm and does the necessary steps to impregnate a woman. I have already been thinking about it, doing research, and preparing for this option. I would rather be in a relationship of course and have a child that way, but if life does not work out for me in that way, then this is my plan B option. I am sure I will cause a lot of controversy with my friends and family, but everyone who knows me well, knows that having a baby in this life is very important for me. I do not want to give up that dream to experience this life with my own child to raise, love, and take care of.

Dating men with children is an experience within itself. Mr. Ex-Fiancé had four children by three different women, three of them were legally his, and the other was from one of his ex-wives that he took in as his own. I became close to all of the children, and the hardest part was walking away from them. Not only did I lose him, but I also lost the children, in which one was already calling me mommy. This was extremely heartbreaking. Words cannot describe what it felt like to have to give up taking care of those children that became a huge part of my life. I went from having those children in my life to being alone, and that was the hardest thing ever – to get used to silence again and to not have anyone to cook or clean for and look over after. Dating someone with children is a situation that needs to be taken with caution and care – to not get the children involved in the relationship too early.

Another issue in the opportunity to have a child is some men may not want any more children. They may feel like the ones they are raising are enough for them. Some men also have already had a vasectomy and cannot have anymore. So not only am I looking for Mr. Prince Charming, but I am also looking for Mr. Prince Charming That Wants To Have A Child. Wow, can finding this type of man get any more complicated for me? And can my title for my man get any longer? Let's hope not for the sake of the readers.

To have a child in this world is a true blessing. I want to know and feel what it is like to be a mother. Not only that, I want to raise a child and have that special bond that mothers have. Something that everyone should cherish and definitely not take for granted. Children do require a lot of love and attention, and we as adults must have what it takes to support the love and attention they need before bringing one up in this world. Having a child is truly a wonderful and fulfilling phase in a woman's life.

CHAPTER 9

Self-Esteem Sinking

I UNLOCK MY APARTMENT door and turn on the lights. Other than Mo greeting me, I sit down on my couch and listen to dead silence. A stillness that lets me know I am the only human existence in the room. No one to have communication with, absolute silence. Friday night and alone again, I think to myself. I sit down on my couch and wonder what I will do with my solitude weekend. Negative thoughts race through my head. When will my life change? Why am I always alone? How am I going to survive another weekend on my own? Too upset to even cry, I look around trying to find an ounce of comfort to offer relief to my state of loneliness.

Did I shave my legs this morning in the shower? Did I bother to eat healthy? Did I work out? Did I go tanning? The answer is no. I have been single for so long and have developed a sense of who I am as a single woman. I tend to let things go, bringing negative energy into my life. If I do not have someone to impress, then what's the point, right? If I do not have someone to make me smile and bring love into my life, then why try?

That was my way of thinking until I woke up and realized that a man does not make me who I am. A man does not justify what or how I should look. I should only be doing things for myself and activities that make me happy and feel good. Since I have been single, I have to admit that I have been letting myself go. The morning came, that I couldn't button my size 8 jeans and when I started wearing a girdle, yep, I said it and did it, a girdle with my work clothes so my belly did not spill out over my business attire. I stepped nervously on the scale to see a number that I have never seen before. That is when I realized that I needed to start taking care of *me*. I needed to be selfish for once and do what's best for *me*. I needed to stop being down on myself about being single and realize that I can be happy on my own.

So I deleted all the online dating prospects from my phone and realized I needed to be free from the Web dating world. The Web dating world was hindering me. I was spending way too much time on the internet searching profiles when I needed to be jogging with my dog Mo. I needed to be out and joining the world and not staring at a screen and talking to men online who may or may not be real or who they say they are. I realized my world was centered on trying to find a man rather than centered on doing what makes me happy and taking care of me.

Being confident can be very, very sexy. When a man sees a self-assured woman who knows what she wants and who has a smile on her face, that is the kind of woman most men want. And that is the kind of woman that I wanted to see in myself again. Not because men want me to be, but because it will overall just make me feel better. Once women start to lose that confidence but continue to date, men can see that. Men can tell if a woman is not happy with herself and who she is, and that makes them nervous. Most men want a self-assured woman in their lives.

I also found myself being in a bad mood after blind dates. Why? Because the person I was with, one or two things would happen. I either did not want to be with him because I knew I was not interested within the first thirty seconds of meeting, or I would like him and he would end up not wanting a relationship. I was participating in an environment that was making me feel not so good about myself, and it was bringing negative energy to my life and my body.

I knew I needed a change to get my life back on track. Once I made that change and stopped focusing on finding Mr. Prince Charming is when I realized that I am fine on my own. I should be proud of all that I have accomplished, and that I can be happy with just knowing who I am as a person. As long as I am happy with me, then I can be happy with anything that life throws me. It is a sigh of relief knowing that I am fine being on my own.

Depression can make a person feel as small as an ant and can really change someone. I know because I have had times where I have gone through depression. Depression took me to a whole new realm in my life that was not a good place to be or a good way to feel. That is why it is important that I do not let single life bring me down. There are positive reasons to being single. Here are a few of my favorites on living the single life.

Living the Single Life # 1

Living by my-self can be peaceful. Not having to share or pick up after someone else can be a very refreshing change in pace. Planning out my day how I want to and not having to check in with someone else.

Living the Single Life # 2

I make my own schedule. I do not have someone clouding up my schedule with more tasks and chores that I already have on my own.

Living the Single Life # 3

I do not have to worry about someone getting agitated in the morning since I am not a morning person. I can be just like Oscar the Grouch in the morning, so I only have me to get on my nerves.

Living the Single Life # 4

I can go wherever I want and talk to whomever I want without having to tell someone else or answer to someone else.

Living the Single Life # 5

I get to have more hobbies. Hobbies are important to maintain my individuality, and this is something I can do as much as I want to without interruption. My hobby, such as writing, I never do when I am in a relationship. In fact I started writing so many times and then would stop when I had a man come into my life.

Living the Single Life # 6

My money is my money. No sharing my money with someone else. No having to budget for two people and spending money when and where I want to.

Living the Single Life # 7

Not being judged for my pick in TV shows. Mr. Ex-Husband couldn't stand some of the shows I watched, such as *American Idol* and *Grey's Anatomy*, to name a few. Now I can watch what I want to watch.

Living the Single Life # 8

No arguing over what to make for dinner. I eat what I feel like eating.

Living the Single Life # 9

Decorating my place how I want it. No smelly guy stuff to deal with.

Living the Single Life # 10

I can act as silly as I want, like singing or dancing around my place without feeling embarrassed.

As you can see, there are many wonderful reasons to embrace the single life. Being single will not last for long even though right now I do not see anything changing, but it eventually will. I will embrace being single, because once I find that one and get a ring on my finger, my single life is done and gone forever. I am then in a committed relationship that should be taken seriously and vows not taken lightly. Being in a relationship is a big responsibility on both persons' part to take care of one another and be there for each other.

So every day, I remind myself of why it is so nice to be single, and it gives me a new perspective on living the single life. Look at all the positive reasons of being single. With that said, I also make sure that I do not remind myself how good it is so that I sabotage myself from ever finding someone. I let my heart be open to someone while being me and being happy with me. Not only will my happiness make a difference to me, but others will see it, and men will start to take notice.

CHAPTER 10

My Dog and Men

"MO SALUTE, GOOD girl." Mo wags her tail with an intensity waiting for me to drop her meaty bone in her drooling mouth that I had just bought for her. She gives me a salute (the best that she can for a dog) and I give her a treat. I sit down on the cool grass on an October day in Texas as Mo busily chews on her bone. She now is in a world of her own chewing her bone. She forgets everything else around her as she happily lay's in the cool grass enjoying her treat. We had just got done with our jog around a lake at a park near our home on a cool, breezy day. Mo growls at any passerby's as she protects anyone from taking her bone. She lay there as she protects her food. She must think that her bone is so good that a human might take it from her. She tries to act tough but looks so cute instead.

Mo, my spoiled 16 pound dog, who is white with black spots, lives a good, carefree, and simple life. I sit there on the grass thinking, how simple my life could be just like Mo's if I would just let it be. If I could just stop worrying so much about the little things in life and instead start enjoying all the little moments that sometimes go unnoticed. The little moments are the moments that are life defining and memorable. I need to slow down just a bit to pay more attention to these little moments. Mo has no idea that although I teach her how to do tricks and such, I equally learn the same amount of lessons from observing her, and her simply being a part of my life. I admire my four legged friend and her strength. Hoping one day, I have as much strength and determination as her.

Pets are a wonderful part of our lives here in the United States. Whoever came up with the idea of having pets as part of our family and as a profound friend should be recognized. Pets are proven to help adults reduce stress, be there as a companion, and give us a sense of security, even though Mo would probably just lick an intruder instead of bite an intruder. It is true what they say about dogs being a man's best friend.

Growing up as a child, I have always had a dog as a pet. I have always had one that has been my friend. I would always have one of my furry animals when I went jogging, roller blading, came home from a long day, or one to curl up at my feet. I have had a cocker spaniel named Annabelle, a German shepherd named Shepherd (very original huh?), and all of the bird dogs my grandfather had while I was growing up from a child into an adult. I hold very good memories of my pets. The dogs that have been in my life became a friend and family to me and will always be remembered.

One day when my Mr. Friend-with-Benefits (remember that jerk from my earlier chapter) came over and told me to help him get the dog hair off his back before leaving to go home. He, in a frantic motion tries to get the hair off of him before leaving my apartment. I chuckled to myself. I told him that I think he would survive the drive to his apartment with a little bit of dog hair on him. I knew he would never find a fit in my life. Someone who is perfect and neat doesn't mix well with a country gal like me. Yes, Mo sheds, and I do my best to keep my apartment hair-free, but sometimes being a pet owner, it is a fact that being hair-free is unavoidable, especially when you own a jumping jelly bean, I like to call my Jack Russell.

My Jack Russell, her name is Mo. She is just like my child, and if a man does not like her or if Mo doesn't like him, well, that is the end of that relationship. Mo tells me a lot about people, and I listen to her. She has an intuitive sense as a dog that I do not have. She is not only my friend and family, but also my protector. I truly believe that she knows when a person is of good intentions or bad intentions. She is my sixteen-pound child that gets love and attention from me as well as gives me the same. If dogs are allowed, then she goes with me anywhere that I can take her. She is getting older now. She is almost eight. Her birthday is in February, just a few weeks before mine. She is my bundle of joy that lights up my life.

Owning my first dog when I was married was like having our first child or, well, as close as I was going to get since Mr. Ex-Husband did not want children during the time we were together. After Mr. Ex-Husband and I decided we wanted a dog to add to our craziness, I started doing some research so I could make sure I found the perfect dog to add to our family. Mr. Ex-Husband had family who had a Jack Russell, and I just loved that little dog. So I bought a book on Jack Russell's and decided that Mr. Ex-Husband and I could handle one.

Mo, my Jack Russell, I found her for sale in the newspaper. Mo's mom was an award-winning agility short-haired Jack Russell, and Mo's father was a long-haired Jack Russell. When we went to pick her out, I picked her because I thought she was the prettiest out of the litter. Mr. Ex-Husband, however, did not have the same opinion. He said, "That dog is way too hyper out of all of them, what are you thinking?" I told him I wanted the pretty white one with the brown patch over her eye. He was not happy that instead of looking at the personalities, that I chose Mo based on being the best looking. Well, of course I won that battle and picked her. She is beautiful, but, boy was she a handful as a puppy!

She hated thunderstorms, and we lived in Alabama at the time, in which we had a lot of them. So every time she heard thunder, she would try anything she could to get out of the house. One time we got home to one of our doors, the bottom of it torn apart, and her teeth bleeding due to chewing the door over her nervousness of thunderstorms. She definitely was a handful, and at times the thought crossed our minds of why we decided to get a dog. I never knew owning a puppy would be so hard to train. As a puppy, she cost us quite a bit of money due to her mass destruction during storms and chewing shoes, clothes, furniture, and well, everything.

Although she was a lot to deal with at first, she brought happiness to our lives and became a wonderful part of our family. She taught me maturity on so many levels. She taught me life lessons that I never knew a dog could teach me. She taught me patience and how to be a better person. Although she was a handful, she was our child who at times would bring Mr. Ex. Husband and me together when times were rough. Lesson learned: all couples should own some sort of pet.

She is a very unique Jack Russell. Mr. Ex-Husband and I had so many ups and downs with her as a puppy. She ate material things especially shoes. She liked to chew and gnaw furniture and walls in the house. So we finally put her in the Pet Smart puppy training class. After that, Mo was finally house-trained, and she learned how to sit, lie down, shake hands, and even salute. We learned how to train her not to chew things, and to be a house dog. That was a sigh of relief once we got her house-trained. We no longer had to hold our breaths while we were gone, wondering what she has gotten herself into or scared to open the door when we arrived home. Instead she would greet me at the door and wait for me to pick her up and give her all the attention in the world, like I still do to this day.

Now that she is older and been through a lot of life changes with me, she has tamed down a lot. When people meet her, they always say, "Wow, that is one hyper dog." I always tell them no, not anymore, she is a lot calmer than she used to be. She also has slowed down even though most people do not notice like I do. Do not get me wrong, she still is very active and runs faster than a fly on steroids, she just has tamed down a bit and became a young adult right before my eyes. I can tell she has gotten older. She has more whiskers now and looks older in the face. She still keeps up with me when I take her jogging. She also still enjoys chasing every squirrel that she sees. Although I often wonder if the reason for that is because, I too, have gotten older and possibly slower. I guess we are aging together through the twists and turns of life.

Introducing Mo to could-be Mr. Prince Charming is always eye opening for me. If Mo and Mr. Prince Charming do not like each other, then I have to call the relationship off. She is my child that will always be a part of my life until death does us part, so whoever I am with must love my Mo as much as I do. If she barks at Mr. Prospect at first, then that is normal, but if she won't stop barking at Mr. Prospect, then she doesn't like him. When Mo is interested, trying to get Mr. Prospect's attention and sniffing him, then that is a good sign that she likes him. But if Mr. Prospect does not like her or is mean to her, well, he is done for, kicked to the curb, and I am on to the next. That is just as bad as being mean to me if Mr. Prospect is mean to Mo.

You can see that Mo and I have a close bond to where my man will not only be dating me, but also dating Mo. I am sure that all you single mothers out there can relate to this as well. Just like if a woman has a child, as a mother she protects and is careful to whom she lets into their lives. Mothers have to be careful of whom and when to introduce their child or children to other people. Children do not understand when people leave out of their lives, and that is definitely a hard task for mothers. Mothers not only have to think of themselves, but also about the ones they are protecting from getting hurt.

Mo, although she is a furry dog, and just a pet, will always be counted as a child of mine and my best friend. Mo provides me with companionship and someone to care for as I am living alone.

She is more valuable than she realizes. She passes judgment on all men she meets, and I am glad she does. She keeps me in-line when she knows that someone just is not right for me. Mo has lived with me for many years now, and she knows me well. She cannot talk, but her face and expressions say it all, and that is all I need from her to help me through my dating phase of life.

CHAPTER 11

What I Have Learned

ANOTHER SATURDAY MORNING, I wake up, feeling refreshed, renewed, and at peace with my-self and who I am. I get up and pour myself a cup of coffee and walk out to my patio and sit in my patio chair. With my positivity and new outlook on life, I sit in the peace and quiet enjoying the breeze and sun shining down on me. I am no longer covering my head with a blanket and hiding from the world. I am no longer afraid of family and friends that do love me as I was before because of all the hurt and pain I endured within relationships. Instead I am enjoying every minute of life and finding joy among the small things in life and my surroundings.

From the journey of going from being in relationships to being single, I have learned a great deal of what not to do. I am definitely not a person to write a self-help book, but if I were, it would all boil down to one fact, which is, there are no rules to dating. When it comes to dating, rules complicate life. Men are already so complicated and hard to figure out, so why should woman add anymore complication to the mix? Rules just make it tougher to fall in love with someone if us, women are trying to follow some guideline or rule book.

Women can read articles after articles on topics such as: what to do on a first date, what to wear on a first date, when is it right to have sex, or how long a person should wait to be boyfriend/girlfriend status. The heart knows and if women all take some steps back to just listen to what the heart is saying and what the heart really wants, she will then know which direction to go. A woman knows when someone is right for her and when someone is wrong for her. When she knows someone is wrong for her, she cannot keep that person in her life as a Mr. He Could Change into What I Want, because he won't, and it will only bring negativity to her life by keeping him around in a potential Mr. Prince Charming status.

I have learned to take care of me first and then a relationship will follow. Taking care of me is important to not only bring confidence, but also self-gratification, and knowing I am fine being on my own. Instead of trying to find a date for a movie or for an event that is coming into town, I go by myself. I figure I have just as much luck having a good blind date as I would have running into someone at a movie or event. I have decided I would rather run into someone than to plan a date I have to stress about.

Being single is not the end of the world. Sometimes it feels like it though, especially after a bad date gone wrong or when I go to bed at night and realize night after night I am alone. I have learned if I do not dwell on the past and I learn that loneliness is something that is only temporary, that helps me get through the negative thoughts of being single. Even if being single is what is meant for me for the rest of my life, then I know that I will accomplish great successes without a man by my side.

Being single is the time to make new friends and get out more. Who knows, I may even meet someone when I least expect it, as friends and family tell me. Single women out there, just remember, being single will not last forever, so enjoy it while it lasts. Being single can be fun and is a part of our lives that woman will always remember, so single women might as well live to make good memories to look back on – memories that will stay with them forever and that they can tell stories about. Personally, I would rather spend my money on going out and having a memory than spending money on material possessions. Good and bad memories are what make us into who we are. Our memories are what make us our own unique selves.

Being in the single status feels like it will last forever, but I can assure *you* being single more than likely will not. We are all people who have a need to be with someone, and we all will run into that someone when the timing in our lives is right. The single life is something that should be cherished and held dear to our hearts. I get to go out and do what I want and go out with whom I want to without being questioned. I do not have to tell anyone where I am or ask anyone if it is okay what I do. I have absolute complete freedom and control over my life and creating who I am as an individual. Being single gives me a chance to be independent and take care of myself.

Being independent is a feeling in itself that is so deliberating and free. When I am in a relationship, I do not give myself full attention. I concentrate on the other person and pleasing the other person that I overlook myself and my needs the majority of the time. When I over look my feelings and my needs, I lose some of my positivity and drive. This is the time to take care of me and do things that I want to do. This is my time to be a little bit selfish, concentrate on me, and get to know myself better. When I do not have anyone to talk to except for myself, yes, on occasion I do talk to myself (and, well, Mo), then I learn more about myself, who I really am, what I really like, and what I want out of life.

There is no better time for soul-searching than while I am single. Things are not always what they seem. This is a true statement I have learned. I can be looking at my point of view in one way, while the person I am in a relationship with has a complete opposite point of view on a matter. People say words that they do not mean. People think thoughts that I do not know what they are thinking. Sometimes people have an alternate plan for what they really want. I think a man sometimes wants something to be a certain way, when in reality the woman does not. Sometimes the thoughts I do not say are what hurt the other person the most. I do not think that we as people mean to hurt people, but sometimes this does occur.

All I can do is protect my heart and hope for the best. But I also have to be careful to not guard my heart so closely that I do not let others in. I also need to remember to respect others and to not play games. When it comes to love, playing mind games is not something that will end up leading to happiness. I do not want men to play games, so I should not either. Just because men do something or think a certain way does not mean that I have to. I will stick to what I believe in and not let someone sway my way of thinking if I have a strong stance on a particular subject. Also, I tell myself to be smart, and if situations start happening in a relationship that does not feel right, than the situation probably is not right. I do not just stay in a situation because it is comfortable or I am scared of where my life will go if I leave. I always listen to what my heart is telling me because my heart will always be right. My heart will guide me through the times that I am not sure what path in life to take.

I keep my attitude in check. A negative attitude is the number one reason that will bring me down. When I have a bad attitude about how my life is going, a few extra pounds gained, a negative comment a stranger made to me, a bad day at work, or anything that might come my way, then my whole day, or even week, is ruined. I try and make my attitude strong enough to fight against negativity. Even if I have to tell myself when I have a bad attitude to not have a bad attitude, then I do it. Yes, I do talk to myself, which may be on the border line of crazy, but it helps me to sort my thoughts. When I am positive and I shake negativity off, that is what will make all the difference. Having a positive attitude definitely makes the difference between having a bad day and having a good day. The good days are always better.

The ultimate lesson I have learned about being single is a man does not determine my happiness. If I am not happy with my life and how life is going, adding a man to the picture does not solve the problem, it just adds another person into the mess of me not being happy. I will not make a man happy if I am not content. My low self-esteem will show through, and that usually will make a man uninterested. Self-esteem and the way I feel about myself makes a big difference of how I come across to others. Day-by-day I place emphasis to never lose my self-worth and always feel good about the person I am. If I do not, then there is some serious soul-searching that is needed. I have noticed that when I put all my energy into something, then that is the result I get, so if I am thinking negative thoughts, such as I am fat, I am not as smart as I would like to be, I am single and alone, then those are the results I will get. When I feed my brain negative energy, then my brain is going to think that is what I want, and I will be stuck with negativity. I feel it is important to always try and have positive thoughts. Although negative thoughts are unavoidable at times, but when those negative thoughts come flooding in, I try and get into the habit of adding something positive to the negative thought that entered my mind. It makes a world of difference on having more good days in life than bad days.

Happiness does not come from only within like everyone says. It is up to me to create my own happiness. So, single ladies, let us pat ourselves on the back for having the chance to live the single life and surviving it. Feel good about being a woman and embrace life, even all of the struggles. I know that I am not perfect, and I still struggle with finding the one perfect relationship that is right for me and perfect for me. But I keep going, and I am determined not to give up. I have a small molecule of hope left within my heart that I am holding out for.

So single ladies, define who *you* are and what *you* stand for to keep *you*rself grounded. Always remember that there will be some bad and lonely times, but there will also be some fun and adventurous times. Just keep on living and keep on being *you*. Because in the end *you* is what *you* really have and what *you* will always have. *You* are what make this world unique, and *you* add something to this world that no one else can. We all do. So remember *you*r uniqueness, and if a guy does not like who *you* are, then move on to the next guy. Just remember, there are no rules to dating with the exception of being safe and smart while doing it. Just keep in mind, take it slow, be confident, and if in doubt, he is out! Follow *you*r heart, and *you* will find what *you* are looking for.

POEMS
OF A
SINGLE WOMAN

Poem on Loneliness

Loneliness

Day after day I struggle with being alone and do not know which direction to find happiness anymore.
I wonder if I will ever find what I am looking for.
I think of how men have hurt me in the past and wonder if I really want one or not.
I do not want a repeat, and it might not be worth taking another shot.
Every year I age and I might not get my chance to have a baby of my own.
But with the world and how people treat one another, maybe it might be best that I let go of this dream, to not bring someone else in the world to hurt and to be alone.
I want to be happy, and I want to be content, so I can show the world the real me.
But loneliness has consumed me and all that I am worth, so tonight I just let it be.

These three are in memory of Mr. Ex-Husband

Which Way to Turn

Why do I feel so lonely when I am not lonely at all?
How do I decide what is best for me, how do I make that call?
Why do I make it so difficult for him to love me?
Making vows to always and forever love, somehow I lost sight of us and cannot clearly see.
Why does loving you have to be so tough for us these days?
Every night I go to sleep and pray it is just a phase.
I cannot leave; I cannot love, so what am I supposed to do?
I wish I could freeze time to figure out what I am to do with you.
Questioning myself every day why our paths crossed in each other's life.
Thinking back into the past, trying to remember what made me want to be your wife.
I do not know which way to go; I do not know which way to turn.
Oh please someone help me, for the truth I need to learn.

Trying to Move On

What do I do when the relationship is all said and done?
When I know that it was partly my fault, so how do I live, how do I go on?
We fell in love from the very beginning when we started to date.
I did not want to be without you, I wanted you with me at all times. How quickly everything changed, now I am left alone to deal with my own fate.
I loved you so much that I did not realize too much love pushed us both away.
I moved out, got an apartment, thinking he will realize what he is missing since I felt neglected but instead I just pushed him away without letting him have a say.
When that did not work, I got divorce papers, thinking this will surely do the trick.
Instead he signed them with the last thought being that I am crazy.
Maybe I am, maybe I am not, but I know this has made me sick.
Now I am left to ponder my life and how I must change.
He taught me a valuable lesson to help me rearrange.

Broken

Our marriage is broken, there has been too much that has been said and done.

We both are now faced to move on with our lives with the next step being a divorce so it can be set in stone.

Let's move on for both of our hearts are broken and torn.

Let's move on and stop fooling ourselves, for the devil has invaded our lives, and he has won.

We both have done so many things to hurt one another out of loneliness.

I hope one day we can look back, remain friends, and both find happiness.

The Ex-Fiancé

Trouble

I wake up in a hospital trying to remember what made me get in my vehicle and drive myself here.

Then I remember what happened to cause this, and wonder how in the world I got myself wrapped up in trouble that made my life so complicated and living in fear.

I knew I had to change the situation I was in and run and get away. So that is what I did, I started a new life in a new state for a new start in high hopes of turning my life around from the price that I had to pay.

Starting over was the best decision I ever made.

Now I am right where I need to be, I was able to let go of the past and let it fade.

Friend with Benefits

Walking Away

The romance started off with holding hands, then a kiss, then an undeniable passion that both of us felt.

We both kept coming back for more over and over until you started making my heart melt.

Then I told you I loved you even though that was not part of the deal.

It ruined everything we had because you claim you do not know how to have emotions, and you did not want anything real.

Such a fool, such a fool was I to keep coming back for more because it felt so right.

Such a fool, such a fool was I to keep getting hurt over and over again just to be close to the person I knew was a losing battle that I could not fight.

Now you keep trying to stay in touch with me since I walked away.

If you cannot ever love me then please go, you are the one who chose the price, now it is time for you to pay.

ABOUT THE AUTHOR

L.M. Grimes was born and raised in Nacogdoches, TX. She spent 8 years on active duty and still serves the military in the reserves. She now works for a well-known University and resides in the Dallas-Fort-Worth area at current. She has always enjoyed writing. Writing notes, putting thoughts on paper, poetry, and now, putting her thoughts in books. She wants to look back on life without holding back, without having secrets from the rest of the world. She wants her readers to read her writings and get to know the view of a single woman within this book. This is her, being real, being true to herself, and exposing a part of her words for others to find inspiration and laughter.